B53 037 499 8

D0505424

DIARY OF A FLY

WORM'S CAP IS RED
MOULDY CHEESE IS SO BLUE
I LOVE MY MUM
AND SHE LOVES ME TOO!

BE MY VALENTINE!

Valentine card for Mum.

FLY GIRL

Worm chewed this for me.

My bows!

Great-great-grandmother with
baseball player Babe Ruth!

Skywriting with Worm.

Me as a baby.

Found this cool meteorite.

For Cory and Jessica
—D.C.

For my beautiful niece, Maddy. I love you.
—H.B.

Diary of a Fly. Text copyright © 2007 by Doreen Cronin.
Illustrations copyright © 2007 by Harry Bliss.
First published in the US in 2007 by HarperCollins Publishers.
First published in the UK in 2012 by HarperCollins Children's
Books. HarperCollins Children's Books is a division of
HarperCollins Publishers Ltd, 77-85 Fulham Palace Road, London
imprint of HarperCollins Children's
W6 8JB

1 3 5 7 9 10 8 6 4 2

ISBN: 978-0-00-745591-1

No part of this publication may be reproduced, stored in a retrieval
system or transmitted in any form or by any means, electronic,
mechanical, photocopying, recording or otherwise, without the prior
permission of HarperCollins Publishers Ltd, 77-85 Fulham Palace Road,
London W6 8JB
www.harpercollins.co.uk
All rights reserved
Printed in China

DIARY OF A FLY

Written by Doreen Cronin
Illustrations by Harry Bliss

HarperCollins Children's Books

JUNE 7

Tomorrow is the first day of school. I'm so nervous. What if I'm the only one who eats regurgitated food?

JUNE 8

Great news! Everyone eats regurgitated food!

JUNE 10

Things they teach you in flight class:
We are the most accomplished fliers
on the planet.
Our average speed is 4.5 mph.
Leap backwards when taking off.

Things they should teach you in flight class: Always have a flight plan.

ZIP

JUNE 12

My parents left us with a babysitter last night. When they got home, eighty-seven of us were stuck to a strip of flypaper.

WHOOSH

Mum says we were a lot easier to watch before we grew heads.

JUNE 14

Today we practised landing on moving targets.

I am standing on her head right now.

JUNE 15

My school picture came out terrible.

Mum says next time I had better have all my eyes looking in the same direction.

JUNE 17

My first science homework task is to use my five senses to observe something creepy. I chose a year one boy.

JUNE 18

Worm and Spider came over today. We used a magnifying glass to take a really good look at ourselves.

Man, we are FILTHY.

I told her we could put half of them
in the garage to save space.

I'm having a time-out
in the garage right now.

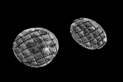

JULY 15

Worm sat me down and explained
the food chain.

That is so not cool.

JULY 16

The babysitter came back last night.
She brought a frog.

When Mum and Dad got home,
we were all exactly where we were
when they left.

JULY 21

Why I would make a good superhero:

I have the most powerful flight muscles on the planet.

I can land upside down.

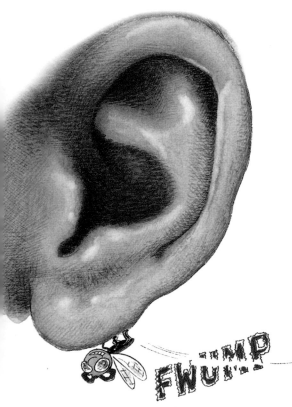

I can see in all directions at once.

Spider said, "Superheroes bend steel with their bare hands. You eat horse manure with your feet."

I never thought about it that way.

JULY 22

Today I learnt that flies beat their wings 200 times per second.

No wonder I keep falling asleep in maths.

AUGUST 1

I just know I would make an excellent
superhero:
I have 4,000 lenses in each eye.
I can walk on walls.
I can change directions in flight
faster than the blink of a human eye.

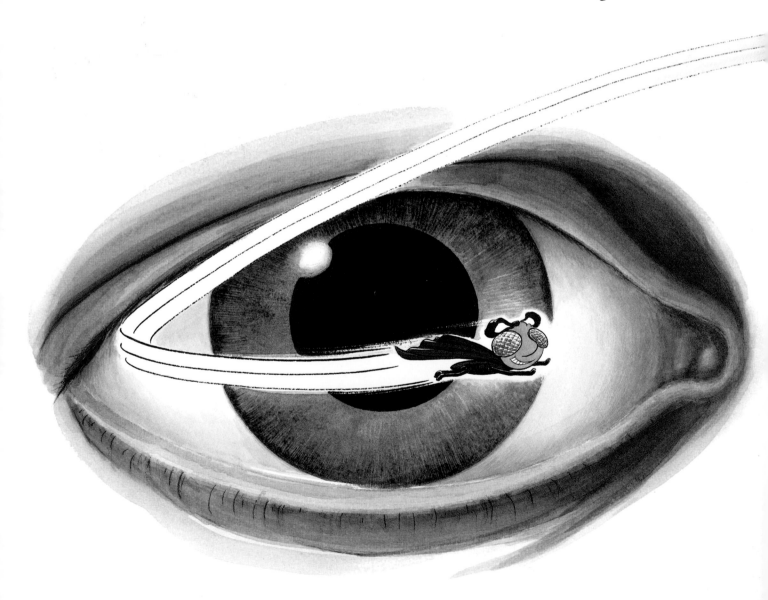

Spider said, "Superheroes save the world from outer-space villains. Your brain is the size of a sesame seed."

I never thought about it that way.

AUGUST 2

Today I told Worm and Spider that
I could never be a superhero like
I wanted.

Worm looked me right in the eyes
and said, "The world needs all kinds
of heroes."

Spider said, "I never thought about it that way."

Neither did I.

Book Report by Fly

LORD OF THE
FLIES
by William
Golding

A
Nice Job!
Next time no
doodles in the
margin.

Mum put this
on the fridge.

Spider is soooooooo
good at football!

Worm tunnelled right
through this marshmallow.

My favourite dinner!

Pretty!